G000019318

WHY CAN'T JIMMY SIT STILL?

Helping Children Understand ADHD

Sandra L. Tunis, Ph.D.

Illustrations by
Maeve Kelly

New Horizon Press
Far Hills, New Jersey

To my son Jack,
whose courage, creativity and compassion
have been inspirational

Copyright © 2004 by Sandra L. Tunis, Ph.D.

All rights reserved. No portion of this book may be reproduced or transmitted in any form what-soever, including electronic, mechanical or any information storage or retrieval system, except as may be expressly permitted in the 1976 Copyright Act or in writing from the publisher. Requests for permission should be addressed to:

New Horizon Press
P.O. Box 669
Far Hills, NJ 07931

Tunis, Sandra:
    Why Can't Jimmy Sit Still?: Helping Children Understand ADHD

Cover Design: Norma Ehrler Rahn
Interior Design: Bradley Ross

Library of Congress Control Number: 2004108079

ISBN: 0-88282-251-9
SMALL HORIZONS
A Division of New Horizon Press

2008   2007   2006   2005   2004   /   5   4   3   2   1

Printed in Hong Kong

Hello there, my name is Michael Lee.
My best friend, Jimmy, is seven like me.

Jimmy loves babies, puppies, music and art,

But best of all Jimmy has a very kind heart.

Jimmy likes to skateboard, play chess and ride bikes.

He's also a cub scout who camps out and hikes.

Though my friend is smart and extra cool,
He has some very big problems at school.

Jimmy squirms and fidgets and moves all about.
When he raises his hand, sometimes he calls out.

Our teacher gives him looks of concern.

She says, "Jimmy, you must wait your turn!"

He can't seem to hear what she tells him to do.

She continues to scold him until she turns blue.

Jimmy yells during recess and gets carried away,
So some of the kids say they don't want to play!

Back in class, when the students are settling down,
Jimmy can't seem to stop all his clowning around.

Sometimes the teacher sends Jimmy out into the hall,
Then his face turns red; he doesn't like it at all.

My friend wants to behave, to pay attention, too.
Although he tries, these are things he just cannot do.

He says stopping his wiggling is hard as can be,
Because Jimmy just cannot settle down, you see.

He has a "motor" inside that is stuck in high gear.
When other kids laugh, Jimmy loudly will cheer!

Last week when his grandfather came to town,

Jimmy's huge hug almost knocked Grandpa down!

Getting ready for school each day is a chore.

Jimmy is too slow and has to rush out the door.

Homework is a challenge each and every day.

Jimmy's many daydreams often get in the way.

Doing assignments seems so easy for others,

His classmates, his friends and even his brothers!

Jimmy is confused and feels angry and sad.
He is starting to think that he is just bad.

He overhears the neighbors say, "That behavior's a shame!
Why, it must be the boy's parents who are to blame."

That day Jimmy goes home with a tear in his eye.

His mom sees his sadness and asks, "Why do you cry?"

Jimmy shakes his head, "I have too much behavior, you see.

Some people laugh and scold and make fun of me."

She sits down next to her son and reaches for his hand,
"People can say mean things when they don't understand.

"You are a very good boy whatever they say.
You just have a problem that gets in the way."

"We all need help," his dad adds, "With something or other.

It's true even for grown-ups like me and your mother.

"Being unable to sit still is hard indeed,

But we'll find an answer. We know you can succeed!"

Then Jimmy's mom gives him a kiss on the cheek
And tells him, "We'll go see a doctor next week."

When he goes to the doctor, the man doesn't even frown
At Jimmy who is fidgeting and acting like a clown.

Yes, the doctor is nice; they all talk for a while.

Jimmy's mom is less worried; he can tell by her smile.

The doctor talks about ADHD

Jimmy then wonders, "Is that about me?"

"Some kids have trouble with a 'switch' that's inside,
And to control their behavior they just need a guide.

"These are great kids, but they find it quite tough
To calm themselves down when enough is enough."

"I know it's hard to bring yourself to a halt,
But remember that ADHD isn't your fault."

The doctor looks at Jimmy and gives him a wink,
Then turns to his mother, "We can help your son, I think."

"Kids with ADHD need extra help, you see,
But at home and at school, teamwork is the key."

They make plans that help Jimmy find new ways to behave;
Before long the teachers and children give Jimmy a rave!

With Jimmy's hard work and the help that he needs,
He makes better choices and so he succeeds.

He doesn't jump up and down when he should sit.
Jimmy can wait for his turn without throwing a fit.

He believes in himself, in other kids too.

He's proud of his friendships, some old and some new.

Now that you know him, I'm sure you can see

How brave and special my friend Jimmy can be.

If you meet a boy who acts like Jimmy once did,
I know you won't make fun of that extra-special kid.

Some kids can't help it if they jump up and down,
Squirm or make funny faces just like a clown.

They just have a challenge called ADHD
And need special help with their behavior, you see.

Remember to smile, for in the end,
You could, like me, be meeting your best friend.

TIPS FOR KIDS WITH ADHD

1. Children with ADHD have *problems controlling certain behaviors.* They may have trouble paying attention and sitting still. If you have ADHD, this may be creating problems for you at home and at school.

2. Remember that you are a good person. Children with ADHD are *not trying to misbehave.* You are not "bad" or "stupid" and it is not your fault (or anyone else's) that you have this condition.

3. You don't have to handle ADHD alone. Ask for help from parents, teachers, counselors or others. Your parents may take you to a doctor or other person who is trained to help children with ADHD.

4. Remember that things can get better! Doctors and others have found many ways to help children and parents manage ADHD.

5. Older kids may want to read about ADHD and learn some ways that other young people with ADHD have learned to handle school, friends and family.

6. Some people have a hard time understanding children with ADHD and may make unfair judgements. When you meet people who criticize the way you act or speak, you may feel confused, frustrated, angry or sad. This is understandable and okay.

7. Try to share your thoughts and feelings with your parents and other adults you trust. You will feel better and they will be able to help you get through difficult times.

8. Don't let the opinions of others prevent you from knowing what a great kid you are. Many children and adults with ADHD are smart, creative and fun to be around. Know that you deserve to be recognized for your strengths and abilities.

9. Try to notice which situations seem the hardest for you. They might include meeting new friends or playing games at recess. Take some extra time beforehand to prepare. For example, you might remind yourself that others expect you to wait your turn and will probably yell or criticize you if you don't.

10. Make up special plans to help manage your time. For example, you or your parents might write notes to help you remember to finish homework or chores and put them on a bulletin board or calendar. Select school clothes and pack supplies the night before, so you won't have to rush around in the morning. Talk with your parents about what plans might work best for you and your family.

11. Know that you are not alone. Many, many other kids, teens and adults have ADHD. Talk to other people who have ADHD. They can help you feel less alone.

12. Every day of your ADHD journey, try your very best to control your behavior. Feel proud of yourself when you do, especially when you reach one of your goals. Look to the future with hope and confidence!

TIPS FOR PARENTS

1. Children with ADHD tend to respond quickly and strongly to everyday events. Be aware that they need your help and support managing current activities and planning ahead.

2. Remember that children with ADHD are not "bad" or "undisciplined" and there is nothing their parents or anyone else has done to cause the condition.

3. Seek help from experts in the field. You can start by contacting a pediatrician, counselor, therapist, social worker, psychologist or psychiatrist. You may wish to involve a team of health professionals to help assess your child and develop a comprehensive treatment plan. Teachers may be able to help you identify treatment professionals.

4. Remain hopeful and determined. Many types of treatment (e.g., behavioral therapy or medication) are available. The right treatment or combination of treatments for your child can help him or her successfully manage ADHD at home and at school.

5. Continue to learn about ADHD so that you can better understand what your child might be experiencing.

6. Support your child when others are critical. Let him or her know that for children who frequently face the negative reactions of others, feelings such as confusion, frustration, anger or sadness are understandable.

7. Encourage your child to share his or her thoughts and feelings with you. Be on the lookout for signs of depression and be ready to consult a professional.

8. Make a point of appreciating your child as a whole person with special strengths, qualities and interests. Many children with ADHD are bright, creative, spontaneous and just plain fun to be around. Be generous in complimenting them.

9. Notice which situations are especially hard for your child (e.g., transitions from one activity to another, meeting new friends or unstructured play with several children). Take some extra time beforehand to be a coach.

10. Provide clear expectations and structure for your child's activities. Include plenty of opportunity for success in reaching goals. For example, you might organize an overwhelmingly large school project into smaller, more managable tasks. After each smaller task is completed, provide a rewarding activity such as watching TV or playing outside for a few minutes.

11. Be assured that you are not alone. Many, many parents and children face the challenges of ADHD. Take advantage of opportunities to talk with others who have walked in your shoes. You may find it helpful to contact Children and Adults with Attention-Deficit/ Hyperactivity Disorder (CHADD) at 8181 Professional Place, Suite 201 in Landover, Maryland, 20785. The can be reached at (800) 233-4050 and at www.chadd.org.

12. Every day of the ADHD journey, encourage your child to try hard, to feel proud of his or her accomplishments and to look to the future with strength, confidence and eager anticipation.